The Trapping

Jasmine Hill

DEDICATION

To those who were brave. Who spoke up. Who were heard
by the Inherently Respected loud and clear, gagged, and
discredited as emotional. To those who used to believe in
the system. Who used to believe that if they only found the
right set of ears with the right kind of power, they would
find some sympathy – some justice. This is the writers
clumsy attempt to plant a seed. To open minds to the idea
that justice is only as blind as our preconceptions are
nonexistent.
This small work is dedicated to you. To those of you that
ran out of options. That ran out of fight. That could only
scramble away bleeding and start anew. Whose stories are
scraped off and rewritten by the Inherently Respected.
This is for you.

Contents:

ACKNOWLEDGMENTS

Cover Art by Daniel Perez

CHAPTER 1

"Any room is fine. I'm only hoping to be here a night or two," said Walter Higgins, shifting his weight to one leg and resting a melancholy elbow on the front desk. He was a young man with a slight build and old eyes – the care of several lifetimes robbing something from his otherwise well-proportioned features.

"I'm sorry," said the desk clerk. "Ugh, which room now?"

"It really doesn't – just, any room. Any room is fine."

"Next to me Joe," said a cheery, female voice from somewhere nearby. "Put him next to me."

"Sure thing, Liza."

Walter looked to see who had managed to rouse the desk clerk into responding so quickly. Blue fabric

1

draped over the subtle curves of an ideal female form to his right. Liza smiled and stuck out her open palm. He took it.

"Welcome aboard."

"Ugh, thanks. Nice to meet you... Liza?"

Liza chuckled, "That's me. And your name?"

"Walter."

"Well Walt! Glad to meet you too! You're not from around here."

"No. I'm just passing through. I was on my way to take a new job and my car broke down."

"Oh, how awful! How did you get out here? Did you walk?!"

"No. Fortunately I was near town – the one with no place to stay apparently. But I could schedule car repairs and the shop owner gave me a ride here. I have to say I was surprised..."

"By how far away it is? Yeah, we're out of the way for sure. But you can't beat the tranquility. The pasture views from my side of the building are to die for."

"Thank you for sharing them."

"I am generous, aren't I? Well, I certainly hope you enjoy your stay Walt." Liza nodded her head towards the desk as she started to flit away. "Joe's got your keys I think."

Walter looked back at Joe who was dangling the keys very close to his face.

"Room 31," he said in a weird, flat voice.

"Ok, thanks."

"She's too good for the likes of you."

Walter glanced over his shoulder to make certain Liza was actually gone before answering with a puzzled, "What?"

"I could see the way you were eyeing her," Joe snarled. "She's too good for you. Can you imagine – her – together with a little runt like you? She'd have to bend down to kiss ya. Don't you go getting any fancy…"

"I don't plan on doing much kissing." Walter tried to keep his voice even, but it was proving difficult. "But it sounds an awful lot like you're describing your own urges."

"Around here we know our place. I *know* I ain't good enough for the likes of her. And neither are you."

Before Walter could form words, a man who had been occupying himself with a newspaper and a cigarette stood up from his corner.

"Really Joe! This is no way to treat guests. Stop wagging your tongue and give the gentleman his key."

Joe sniffed and dropped the key on the desk.

"Here – Walter is it? I'll point you in the right direction. I'm Gene. Gene McGivern."

Gene pat Walter on the back and pointed to the stairs. As they moved further away from the front desk, he lowered his voice.

"You mustn't mind Joe. He's held a torch for Liza since he was wearing knicker-buckers and – well, he doesn't care for newcomers."

"An ideal trait for a desk clerk at an *Inn*."

Gene laughed out loud and wacked Walter merrily. There was something in that laugh that seemed vaguely familiar.

"I'm going to like you! We really don't get many guests around here. No, it's true! Most of us are semi-permanent residents of the hotel. For my part it's a matter of comfort and convenience. I'm one of those boys that got a dreaded 'Dear John' while we were over there, and I'm not exactly rolling in dough."

Walter couldn't help but connecting with both those scenarios and it showed.

"Ah," said Gene, "I see that you'll also fit in well here. We're all in similar ships – waiting for life to realize we've been through too much in the past few years to keep getting kicked in the shin."

"Liza too?"

"Oh yes. She doesn't talk much about it. She was a WAC – but she's the most unaffected of the lot of us. Always sweet, helpful and not to mention – I mean you have eyes in your head! But she isn't *that* kind of girl either."

Walter wanted to change the subject. "I'm sure she's swell. Tell me if it's my imagination but I feel like I recognize you from somewhere. I just can't place you."

"Maybe the Army?"

"I was Navy."

"Huh. You seem familiar too, but I didn't have much to do with Navy guys. What about school? Any chance you went to Grove Secondary around '35?"

Walter chuckled, surprised by the coincidence. "As a matter of fact…"

"No kidding!"

It turned out that Gene and Walter had been at the same school for two years, although not in the same classes. They both felt they must have interacted at recess on occasion but never learned each other's names. The connection was loose but still one that helped Walter feel more relaxed in his unfamiliar environment. Relaxed enough so that when Gene invited him to come downstairs later that evening to meet "some of the guys" he felt slightly less inclined to say no.

"I'll think about it," he said.

"Great! Now, go all the way to the end of the hall and make a left – you'll see 31. See you tonight!"

Walter forgave the presumption. He found his

door and shut it behind him, dropping his small leather suitcase on the floor.

Standing just inside, the bed was to his right against the wall, flanked by a couple of bedside tables and small tiffany lamps. Over the wrought iron headboard hung a needlepoint declaring that home is sweet. Walter let out a single, wry laugh. Straight ahead was the only, surprisingly large window, framed by long, ornate curtains. A chair in front of the window and a dresser across from the bed completed the room.

"It's only for a couple of days," said Walter out loud, as if by speaking, he could make it true.

CHAPTER 2

After dosing fitfully for an hour or so Walter awakened to distant laughter. He remembered Gene's invitation and cursed their feeble connection.

He slicked back his hair and left to follow the sounds of merriment. It led him into a room he had not yet seen where everyone was gathered around a black, baby grand. He met Liza's gaze first, broke it and scanned the crowd for Gene. Gene found him.

"Walter! This is Walter everyone! We were school mates if you can believe it!"

That detail was unusually entertaining for longer than necessary, which gave Walter reason to look for a wet bar. After shaking several sweaty hands, he slipped away to pour himself a whiskey. A blue dress followed.

"You'll have to forgive them. They can be a little boisterous," Liza laughed.

"Oh, I don't… I mean – I was in the Navy."

"Did you keep to yourself there too?"

"Was I keeping to myself?"

"I'm sorry, I didn't mean to presume. I have an interest in human behavior and you just struck me as a loner."

Walter took a sip and shrugged. "Can't really deny that. Oh, can I pour you something?"

"No thank you. Well, one way or another, I'm glad you joined us Walt." Liza smiled and turned back towards the piano where the crowd enveloped her once again.

With some strange compulsion to either avoid disappointing her or to prove her wrong, he moved to join them. He steered away from Gene though and found a friendly looking older face to hover near. He knew he had picked a kindred-enough spirit when a bad rendition of "On the Aitcheson, Topeka and Santa Fe" broke out and neither of them joined the din. At least, he thought so until the guy took the cigarette out of his mouth and poked him.

"I saw you offer Liza a drink. She doesn't drink."

"Ugh, thanks for the tip."

The older man nodded. "I'm Charlie."

"Good to meet you Charlie. My name's – "

"Walter. Liza told me."

"Yeah. Um, how long have you been here Charlie?"

"My whole life. I used to run the hotel. Now I just enjoy it. I leave the running to the younger folks." Charlie chuckled quietly at his joke. "Yep, my Daddy used to run it before me. That was a very different time."

"How long has it been in your family?"

"Just my Daddy before me. He built this place with his own two hands. Wanted a place to settle down after the War Between the States. His brother, my uncle, was here for a while but he wasn't much good to nobody. Sat around all day – his wife and kids were more help. 'Course you know his wife had been married before?"

Walter stifled a yawn. "Oh?"

"That she was. So, his kids weren't really his kids. She was a widow-woman. Respectable. But she was quite a woman. Never did have any kids of his own. My uncle, I mean. He tired of the place and took the family all away after –"

Charlie, who had been so intent on retelling his history, broke off and cocked his head. A hush had settled on the crowd. A single, fresh voice rose in beautiful, clear tones. Liza was sitting at the piano, playing and singing: "I'll be seeing you… …I'll find you in the morning sun and when the night is through. I'll be looking at the moon, but I'll be seeing you."

Not a soul present could help but think of someone they would never see again. Collectively, they paused and listened. And through each note and each word, they mourned and wondered why life was so unfair.

Walter made his way to his room early, mechanically changed and got into bed. The covers were scratchy, and they smelled funny – like old flowers. The moon was bright enough to seep through the curtain and even though he avoided looking at it as he lay awake in his scratchy bed, he could still see her. He saw her everywhere.

Her pink, freckled face scrunched into a wide smile. She giggled and laughed. Then as if superimposed, the sound of laughter sounded more like cries. The cries grew louder until they were wails – wails of pain and fear and desperation. Her face no longer scrunched in a smile but in wide-mouthed agony. He called out to her. He tried to reach her but with every effort he was forced backwards. He redoubled his efforts, screamed louder. If she could at least hear that he was there. At least she might not feel so alone, so scared. "I'm here! I'm here!" he cried. For a second he thought she was responding, but out of her bluish lips came the sound of knocking and banging – not a human sound at all.

He leapt out of bed just in time to see his locked door burst open and several people rush into the room. Liza led them.

"Walt! Are you alright?!" She held his arms and searched him with her eyes. "You were screaming."

"Yes, I'm sorry. I'm fine," said Walter, surprised

to find that his voice was hoarse.

There was an awkward pause as it sunk in that Charlie, Gene, Liza and several others had essentially broken into Walters room for what turned out to be some kind of psychological episode. Liza broke the silence first.

"You know what, Walt, it sounds like you might have a cold coming on. How about I go make you some tea?"

Grunts and nods indicated a mutual consensus about the plan as they all shuffled out, expertly avoiding eye contact.

"I'll be back in just a moment." Liza smiled before gently closing the door behind her.

Walters heart beat forcefully against his ribcage, sending tight spasms up into his throat. He allowed his body to unstiffen and collapse back onto the bed – aware however that Liza would return and he would need to hide his current state once again. He took a few deep breathes, stilled his mind and went to put on his robe. He felt he should at least be somewhat decent if he was forced to entertain a woman in his room. He didn't blame her or the others for being concerned – just himself for concerning them.

At first, he sat in the chair, calculating that sitting on the bed seemed too familiar or vulnerable. Then he realized that doing so would force her to sit on the bed which seemed even worse. Moving back to the bed would mean that she could potentially chose to sit next to him on the bed which would be the worst scenario of all. He finally chose the chair, with the intention that, when she arrived, he would stand and offer it to her, thereupon sitting on the bed himself.

When Liza entered with the tray, his plan worked out perfectly and they were soon settled as comfortably as they could be, with the door open, and only his own inherent awkwardness to overcome.

"Thank you. I really have to apologize. I don't remember this happening before."

"Well, you did give me a start."

"I – I'm very sorry."

Liza smiled. "It's really alright. How's your tea? To your liking?"

"Yes, thank you."

"Your welcome." Liza looked down at her lap, flattened her skirt on her knees, and then brought her hands together in a soft clap. "Who's Margery?"

Walter burnt his lip. "Excuse me - what?"

"Margery?"

"Did I…? I must have said it."

"Screamed it actually."

Walter sighed and shook his head.

"A lover? Fiancé?"

"Oh no. She… well, no slight to her, but my fiancé stopped meaning much to me after Margery. She just couldn't understand why… Well, damn it, I don't know why myself. But I'm sorry. I'm sure you don't want to hear…"

Liza leaned forward. "But I do. And I really think it will do you good to talk about it. I think I mentioned that I make a study out of human nature. We've all been touched by the war in horrible, deep ways and I've always wanted to do my best to listen and help – if I can."

"You're very kind. I'm just not sure that I'm ready to talk about her."

"That's alright. But I really believe it'll be a very good thing for you to talk about it eventually. If you do want to talk, remember I'm right next door." Liza stood and took her cup.

"Oh yes, right. I'm very sorry for disturbing you."

"Nothing to be sorry about Walt! I hope you have a better night's sleep from here on out."

"You too," he replied as she left, acutely aware that she *would* have had a better night's sleep, had it not been for him.

CHAPTER 3

Next morning Walter went downstairs for breakfast. Gene was already having his coffee and browsing the morning paper. He waved Walter over.

"Hope you slept...!" Gene trailed off and picked up on a different subject in an enthusiastic, immeasurable percentage of a second. "Murderer! On the loose! Can you believe it?" He slapped his paper. "As if we hadn't all done enough killing already."

Walter decided to go with the pretense and sat down. "Well, if we've learned anything it's that there are evil people in the world."

"Yeah. Sure are. Anything you want? The funnies are pretty good today. I always go for them first. Put me in a good mood."

"I can picture that. I tend to like the sports columns."

"Perfect – here you go. Already glanced over those so they may be slightly wrinkled. Annette always used to say I was a bear with my papers. Although I never heard her complain about… well…" Gene raised a brow suggestively.

"Annette your girl?"

"She was. Gave me that "Dear John" I told you about. What a looker she was though! All the guys were so jealous. All they had were their pinup girls and I had my very real Annette. But you know what the war did."

"I'm not sure I understand."

"You know – put ideas in girls heads. Like they can just pick up and go and do whatever they please. She was a WAC stationed overseas and met this British guy. They're married now I think."

"Sorry."

"For the best. Hey, I'm comfortable and there's hope – I mean look at Liza."

"Are you and she…?"

"No. No. Not hope for me with her. I just mean she gives me hope that there are still good ones left. She was a WAC, just like Annette, and *she* came home. That's what they all shoulda' done."

Gene paused and his incessant smile gave way to something bitter. He quickly shook it off. "What about your girl? What happened there?"

Walter couldn't help but remember the old adage about misery and was in no mood to indulge it.

"It was amicable. The war changed us both a lot. Can't fault her for that."

Gene looked marginally disappointed. But he lifted his coffee cup as if it were a beer and went back to reading his paper. Walter opened his.

It rained for the rest of the day, which derailed Walters ideas of exploring outside of the hotel. He wanted very much to call into town and see how the repairs on his car were going but he managed to suppress the urge. He had only spent one night and they had told him it would take at least three full days. It didn't benefit him to torture himself and annoy the mechanic.

That night he decided to get into bed early. He found a book he had been wanting to read in the parlor and was determined to lose himself in it. He was not going to think about Margery tonight.

Walter felt pretty good about himself when he realized that he had read five chapters before becoming self-aware again. But then the problem became that he was aware of being self-aware, so he continued to read even though his eyes were feeling very dry.

Next thing he knew someone was shaking him and saying, "It's alright Walt! Calm down! You're alright."

"What? What? Liza? Is that –?"

"Yes Walt. It's me. Here sit up. You feel better

now?"

"Yes. Yes, I'm sorry. Did I wake you?" Walter speech was slurred in a half-paralyzed dream state.

"Walt, you were screaming for her again. For Margery."

"Sorry. I didn't realize."

Liza went around the bed and pulled the chair up to it. "You still seem a little out of it. I'll just wait with you until you're better."

Walter looked at the open door. "Did anyone else hear this time?"

"No. At least I don't think so. I happened to be up still, so I came in pretty quickly. The door was already unlocked so I didn't have to go down to get a master key."

Walter was glad but still very groggy and ashamed that all he remembered last was feeling pride in his ability to conquer these outbursts.

"You need to say what's on your mind Walt."

"I can't."

"You can. You need to. This is just going to keep happening you know. I've seen it before."

Walter wanted to be offended, but he also felt that he couldn't be. It had been him who came out of nowhere and broken up two nights of sleep for a stranger who, without obligation, wanted to help.

"Margery," he said and stopped.

"Take your time."

Liza's tone was so soft and disarming. Walter began again.

"We were stationed in Britain in '44. It was a little harbor town. We knew we were a nuisance and some of us tried to make an extra effort to be friendly with the locals. The kids – they were great kids. I'd always try to have a few candy bars to hand out. I mean you know how it was – some of these kids barely remembered luxuries like that.

"There was this one time I was practically mobbed, and I ran out fast. I was down to my last bar when this little girl – I don't know how old she was, I'm not good at figuring ages – she walked up and asked if there were any left. She had a little brother on each side of her and I told her I was sorry, that I just had the one. She took it and I was thinking, 'how is this girl going to break it into three?' But she didn't. She just broke it into two and handed one half to each brother. I mean, it just struck me. So selfless for such a little thing.

"After that I carried three candy bars with me everywhere, earmarked for that little girl and her brothers. Eventually they knew that if they saw me, they were getting a candy bar. Margery – she started coming down to the harbor asking for me. Not for candy – just to talk. She wanted to know what the States were like. Why we sounded so funny. Did I have a dog at home? You know kid-stuff. She was convinced I knew the King of America and that I could take her to meet him one day in 'my boat.'

"When we got our orders, she cried and made me promise to write. I couldn't help but be fond of the kid. Of course, I promised. But I couldn't actually send any letters to her until we came back, and I could deliver them myself. As often as I could jot down a line or two, I did. When we eventually did get back, I had a nice little packet. I had even drawn some little cartoons.

"We got in and we all saw right away – the town had taken a beating. And it hadn't been long from the looks of it. We all ran through the streets trying to help where we could, setting up a kind of hospital for the ships doctor to work in. All the while I was looking for Margery. Praying for Margery. I was sure she'd be alright. Then I spotted her mother. The boys were with her but not Margery. She was crying, sifting desperately through rubble that must have once been a house. I started working alongside her. And it wasn't long before–" Walter cut off suddenly and his face froze.

"You found her," said Liza.

"Yeah. Yeah, I did. I took her to the doc, but he didn't have to tell me. I knew." Warm, wet tears started streaming down his face and nose. There was nothing he could do to stop them.

"Why? Why is it her? I've seen a lot of death and dying. I saw a good friend of mine go. But it's always her. Always her face. She didn't ask for it. She didn't have anything to do with it. This war. The Nazi's. What did they have against Margery? She just wanted a dog and candy bars and letters."

"Maybe it is because she didn't have anything to do with it," said Liza softly, scooting her chair closer and touching his arm. "It makes perfect sense. You were there to protect people like her. People who couldn't protect themselves. I'm glad you told me. Now I can better help you."

"Please don't bother. I mean, I'll be going soon. I don't want to put you out anymore. I'll go have my room changed in the morning."

"Don't you dare. That's what would put me out, Walt. Thank you for opening up. Just remember I want to help and I'm right next door if you need me."

Walter nodded without any intention of taking her up on the offer. The tears had stopped, and he didn't know how to wipe them away in a manly fashion, so he just stood up.

"Thank you for your kindness and concern Liza."

Liza took the hint and moved towards the door.

"Of course! And remember, I'm right next door. Don't hesitate to knock."

Walter nodded again and tried not to look like he was hurrying her out, even though he was. The moment he closed the door after her, awkward chills ran up and down his spine. He rubbed his hands together in an effort to alleviate the sensation, but it didn't work. For the rest of the night he paced, afraid to fall back asleep and dream. Eventually he wore himself out and slumped to his knees at the foot of the bed, where dreams came anyway.

CHAPTER 4

The next morning Walter consoled himself that he had now spent two nights in the place. He shouldn't have to wait much longer. He decided not to go down to breakfast but instead debated going to the front desk to ask for a different room; one as far away from anyone else as possible.

The first detractor to this plan was Joe. Having to ask anything of Joe was not a pleasant experience. What if he got belligerent? Demanding to know why Walter wanted to change rooms and drawing attention from others. The second problem was Liza. She had been very kind and seemed to want to help him. He didn't want her to feel insulted or that he was ungrateful. The last consideration was, of course, that he would be gone soon. Why risk unpleasantries when, in a few days, the problem would disappear on its own?

On the other hand, he had now roused strangers two nights in a row and the prospect of potentially making it three or four was not something he was prepared to accept.

As he wrestled with himself, he made his way to reception where Joe glared and extinguished a cigarette on the desk.

"Yeah?"

"I need to use the telephone," said Walter.

His car wasn't ready. He knew it wouldn't be.

Walter decided that fresh air would do him good. The day was blue and large cotton candy clouds kept the heat of the sun in check. The hotel was well situated in the landscape. The exterior of the building had that Victorian architecture that everyone was denouncing, but Walter secretly liked. If it hadn't been for the stressful circumstances that landed him here and the terrors that reigned over his nights – he might have been able to enjoy his stay. Outdoors, with the trills of birds and gentle breezes he felt blissfully alone in the world.

But eventually the dark had to come.

There were a few minutes when he seriously considered getting drunk. Giving up control to gain it however was too counterintuitive for him to entertain long. So, he opted for a tall glass of warm milk. His mother had always told him that it helps you sleep. He chose a lighthearted novel from the parlor to go with it, propped up his pillows and slid under the covers.

Walter read for as long as he could keep his eyes

open and longer. There were several times when he opened them to find that his neck was craning forward uncomfortably, and that he had been trying to read the same passage over and over without understanding a word.

A bang startled him, and he sat straight up. The book was gone, and daylight was flooding in.

"Yes!" Walter cried in a victorious hush.

Assuming he had dropped the book on the floor, he glanced over the side of the bed. The floor was dusty but bookless. Somehow, he had dropped it on the nightstand. Or maybe he had placed it there in his sleep. Either way, another night was under his belt and for once it had been uneventful.

Bacon, eggs and toast sounded incredible on the morning of Walters third day. He even felt in the mood to sit with Gene and ask if he had slept well. Gene gave his paper a shake and smiled.

"I'm thinking *you* certainly did. You've got the world on a string today."

"It's a good day."

"Let's hope so! I've got a bet on a horse I feel really good about."

"Um-hmm," said Walter pouring himself a full mug of coffee and cream. "What is there to do around here?"

Gene laughed in his deep way. "It depends on

what you like to do. If you like bird watching, it's your kinda' place."

"No, I mean, you have to get into town sometime. What is there to do?"

"I have to be honest, not much. But I'm taking over my uncles' business, so I take the trip into town once or twice a week. I work mainly on the books – I'm an accountant by day. Would you like to hitch a ride with me?"

"Sure. When are you going next?"

"It's your lucky day."

Gene had said that sarcastically, but Walter felt the truth of it in his bones. He planned to enjoy every moment. He even started thinking that if he showed up in town, maybe it would put pressure on the shop. Or maybe they would walk out, hand him his keys with a smile and say something like "good as new!"

The forty-minute drive into town seemed at lot shorter than the drive out of it had been four days ago. Gene parked in front of a little loan office and gestured around him at the street of businesses.

"Try not to get lost," he said.

Walter chuckled and the men went their separate ways. His first stop was, of course, to check on his car. Someone was doing something to it, but it wasn't done, although they did say that the parts should be in any day. Walter decided that "any day" could just as likely mean tomorrow as anything. Nothing was going to spoil his mood. He walked up and down the street a few times, exchanging nods and smiles with some older folks, before deciding to settle into a little diner. For the first time in a very long time Walter was going to treat himself to some pie. It wasn't as amazing as his mother's, but it was still nicely seasoned. After scraping the plate of filling, he raised a couple of brows by ordering a ham sandwich to go. He just kept smiling. It was a dessert before lunch kind of day.

Down the street a way, he discovered a half glass door with a stair behind it and a small, faded sign that read M-something Booksellers. He ventured up the steep, creaking steps to a small room that smelt of smoke and age. Bookcases of all shapes, sizes and stages of decay lined the walls.

"Hello?" Walter called out in a half-whisper.

"He isn't here."

Walter started.

"Excuse me! Who?"

A woman peaked out from behind a curtain at a window seat that he hadn't known was there.

"Liza! I – I'm sorry. I… You gave me a start."

"I see that. I'm so sorry."

Liza pulled the curtain back and swung her legs around to face him. "I also see that you've found my hiding spot."

"I didn't mean to intrude. I can leave."

"No please don't. It is a bookstore after all. Not a heavily trafficked one but..."

"Did you say the owner wasn't here?"

"Mr. Murphy? Yeah, he steps out all the time. But he never minds people looking around without him."

Liza continued sitting on the window seat facing him and smiled attractively. She had her legs and arms pulled in tightly against herself so that she looked very narrow on the wide seat. Walter wasn't sure what possessed him, but he found himself asking, "May I sit?"

She smiled and nodded.

Walter sat down next to her and for the first time he noticed that she had a very pleasing smell. It somehow made him acutely aware of the space between them.

"Do you come here often?" He said and nearly winced in abhorrence of himself for sounding so obviously flirtatious.

Liza chuckled. "Yes. It's my hole in the ground – or wall in this case. I grew up a middle child in family of nine. So, I tend to seek absolute solitude out of habit rather than necessity."

"I can understand that. I came from a large family too. I was the baby though, so my mom doted on me. I think it almost killed her when I went away."

"Have you gotten to see her much now that you're state-side again?"

"We had a long visit. Then I had to get to work, you know? And they weren't really hiring where I grew up."

"Mothers and sons have such a sweet dynamic. I can very well imagine that yours doted on you."

Liza angled towards him slightly which created more distance between them on the seat but made it so that their knees nearly touched. She looked him in the eye until he felt as uncomfortable to meet her gaze as he did to break it.

"How have you been Walt?"

He knew what she meant.

"Good today. Last night was good."

"I'm glad to hear it. Please remember I'm here to help. Don't hesitate to call on me." She leaned forward and touched his knee. "Anytime."

Walter stood up. "Thanks. I – I appreciate your kindness."

"Of course. Well, feel free to kill time here whenever you like. I'd love to see your friendly face among these old books."

"I'm not sure about that."

"Please don't doubt it."

CHAPTER 5

The air was not quite as sweet on the way back to the hotel. Gene prattled on, providing a kind of white noise for Walters thoughts. For the first time he made the conscious decision to consider and debate what was happening between him and Liza. She was attractive. He had flirted with her. His stomach turned too much to consider any more. He was vulnerable. Weak. That had been all she saw and all she knew of him. She was kind but he hated her attention. He hated to admit that – but he did. Also, he was leaving very soon. None of this nervousness and awkwardness even mattered. He shook his head, externalizing the dialog.

"Sorry!" said Gene, "Didn't mean to offend."

Walter glanced over at his driver who was clearly offended himself and decided not to correct the imagined slight. He did decide however, that he was going to take control of his awkward situation. He was going to be friendly with Liza – acting as if her kindness didn't make him feel uncomfortable. Maybe, if he behaved with confidence, he would start to feel it.

That evening Walter went downstairs to eat dinner. He saw that Liza and Charley were sitting together at a large, round table and made a straight line to join them. Liza smiled at him widely and leaned over towards him to pat his shoulder. "I'm glad you joined us for dinner tonight!"

Walter returned her smile and made a conscious effort to maintain the intensity of it as he greeted Charley. Charley was very focused on his food though and only grunted and nodded.

"I was so glad to see you in town," Liza continued. "It isn't much, but it's got its charm."

"Charm is underrated."

"Ever think of staying?"

"No. Not that underrated."

Liza laughed out-loud. "You're a hoot. Oh, look here! I want you to meet Bill – he's another almost resident here. Bill!" She rose swiftly and hooked Bill by the arm as he passed by. After presenting him enthusiastically to Walter she insisted that they all eat together.

Walter felt pleased with himself. Whatever awkwardness he had imagined could only really exist if Liza were less friendly to other men – and that was clearly not so.

After a pleasant evening, with lively conversation

and better than average fare, he dismissed himself jovially and retired to his room. He smiled through a brisk, cold shower, shaved for the first time in a couple of days, and braved wearing the nightshirt his mother had made for him. As long as he didn't look in the mirror, he could admit to it being very comfortable. Wanting to continue the upwards trend, he decided to round out his night with a few chapters from the lighthearted novel he had started the evening before. He was even contemplating lighting his pipe, which he smoked very rarely, when he heard a soft rap on the door.

It was Liza with a tray. "I'm sorry for the intrusion," she whispered, looking him up and down amusedly, "but I thought I heard you up and figured you might like a night cap."

Walter could think of very little aside from his nightgown which was in full view since he had unwittingly thrown open the door. "I – thank you… Just one moment." He slammed the door again a little bit too aggressively and he could hear Liza chuckling quietly on the other side.

He felt flustered and taken off guard. This late-night visit shook the tender confidence he was trying so hard to muster.

Liza was all smiles when he opened the door again. He flashed a smile back at her but wasn't sure whether that made him seem more or less sure of himself.

"So, night cap?" Liza bounced the tray gently forward and took a couple of swift steps past him. He raised his hand to point the way after the fact.

"What…? To what do I owe the honor?"

"Nothing but a desire to check up on you. You seemed a little off tonight at dinner."

"I did?"

"Nothing anyone else would notice." Liza set down the tray and set herself on the foot of the bed. "Was anything bothering you?"

"No, I mean… Nothing out of the ordinary."

"Ah yes. Margery. Do you still have the pack of letters?"

"Letters?"

"The letters you weren't able to deliver."

Walter glanced at his little trunk involuntarily. Liza tilted her head slightly and her eyes saddened.

"Oh. You carry them with you."

"I can't really do anything else yet."

"Maybe one day you'll show them to me."

Walter half chuckled as if she were joking but she didn't seem to return the sentiment. She smiled sweetly and tapped his bed. He moved towards her. Why did he move towards her? Why could he not think of an excuse or a reason why he should be able to decline without appearing as if he was making more of this scenario than it was? Gingerly he perched himself, not too far as to seem repulsed by her, but far enough away to be far enough away.

"What would you like? I brought whiskey and rum. I'm afraid they were all out of wine – but I've penned you as a man who likes harder stuff."

"I thought you didn't drink."

Liza's mouth became suddenly small. "Who told... How did you know?"

"Nobody – Charlie. I think."

"Oh, Charlie. He's mostly correct. Although I do make exceptions. Charlie is – well, Charlie. I'm sure you've chatted with him enough to know how loose he can be with his opinions. I made myself a cup of tea. So you won't be drinking alone."

"Thanks."

Walter took the glass she handed to him – aware of the little fingers that brushed against his. This was getting out of hand. But what was this? Everything was above board. The bedroom door was open, except that when he looked, it wasn't.

"Let's toast to Margery," said Liza, raising her teacup. Their respective containers clinked, and Walter let the tiny wave of alcohol brush against his bottom lip. Whiskey. He hadn't told her which her preferred. He turned his face to look at hers and found that she was looking back at him. Only one of her delicate hands was cradling her cup. The other lay down at her side – at his side. She smiled and her hand slipped subtly up. Her thumb rubbed against his pant leg twice – very slowly with enough pressure to maintain contact with his skin - before he jumped to his feet.

She kept smiling. She never flinched. "Well, it's getting late I guess." Liza started gathering up the tray. "See you at breakfast."

Walter nodded. Stunned. And as quickly as she had come, she left.

CHAPTER 6

There were no nightmares that night. Walter barely slept. Early the next morning before the break of dawn, he went down to the front desk and waited for the morning paper, which was always Genes' first stop before breakfast.

"Good morning," said Walter as Gene approached, stretching.

"Morning! You're up early."

"Yes."

"See you at breakfast?"

"Yes," said Walter.

Gene's face slowly grimaced into a half smile. "OK then. See you."

Walter nodded, and watched Gene walk away. He

stood there a while longer until Joe's belligerent talk became impossible to ignore.

"Get me the car repair shop on the phone," Walter snapped. Joe had not heard quite that tone from Walter Higgins before and he confusedly obeyed.

The repair shop had gotten the part that they needed, but after they had begun to install it, another equally important part had broken – through no fault of their own. This additional part would also have to be ordered from out of town and would likely take several days to get in. Walter slammed the receiver down without warning. Joe grabbed the telephone silently and moved away from the desk.

Walter went a roundabout way back to the stairs so that he could catch a glimpse into the dining room. There was Liza, her hair bouncing merrily on the back of her neck. He couldn't hear what she said but apparently it was amusing because half the room began to laugh with her. She turned her head slightly so that he could see one rosy cheek, which sent him stealing quickly to his room.

After assuring himself that the door was locked, he sat down on the floor in front of his suitcase and opened it tenderly. Out of the lining he pulled two little packets of papers. One packet was dirty and creased and the other was fresh and white. The first packet he held with both hands and squeezed his eyes shut, as if he were attempting to manifest an image or better yet, a reality that was not his own. But as is most often the case, wishing did not make it so. He put the packets down and sighed and then noticed something odd. Both packets were tied up with a bow. He never tied anything with a bow.

He opened the first packet and laid out each letter around him. Every smeared, misspelled word was accounted for. Then he moved on to his own letters – scribbled out in haste and enthusiasm – oblivious to their final, undelivered state. Two pages were missing.

Walter grabbed his suitcase and emptied it in hopeless desperation.

He checked every letter again. And again.

The pages were gone, and as that realization descended upon him, his lungs began to shrivel. His skin went from too hot to too cold alternately and within a fraction of a second.

Suddenly his collar was too tight. He pulled it away from his throat until threads popped. It wasn't helping. He gasped deeply but there was no deeply. His lungs were tiny. He dropped to his hands and knees. Invisible splinters pierced his hands, his arms, his throat. He couldn't swallow. His throat was filled with the driest sand. He was drowning in dryness. He fought with his tiny lungs – forcing them to draw in whatever air existed. A squeaky cry broke free. Then another. Then a deep, guttural wail. Walter grabbed a pillow with his numb, splintered hands and pressed it against his face as the wails continued to come. They came out of the deep – raw, ragged anger at the horror of death. He looked into deaths hollow eyes and a single word began to repeat, *wrong, wrong, wrong!* His wails turned to sobs. Sobs that contorted his stomach and his body along with it. It was all wrong. All of

the death. All of the grief and the tears. But right now –
right at this moment – he could breathe again. Tears
flowed in a sad relief. There was breath enough for him
finally. For right now.

Walter never went down for breakfast – or lunch
– or dinner. When light, unfiltered by clouds or fog,
streamed into his room on the following morning, there
was a knock at his door. Walter jumped upright in bed,
feeling like he was still getting over a very bad flu.

"Who is it?" he croaked and held his breath.

"It's Gene."

He let it out again. "Just a second."

Walter forced his aching limbs to move, grabbed
his robe and made his way to the door.

"Wow! You look terrible!" said Gene.

"Thank you."

"No, I mean it. Are you ok?"

"Better now."

"You must have come down with some serious
bug."

"Yes."

"Do you want me to bring you something? Water
or something sad like that?"

"No, that's ok. I need to get out of my room anyway. I'll just get dressed and come down. Do you know...? Do you know who's downstairs right now?"

"It's pretty scarce. There's some fair or something in town most everyone has gone to."

Walter nodded to himself. "Ok. I'll be down."

"Alright. See you." Gene sounded as genuinely worried as seemed possible for him and he wouldn't turn completely away until Walter shut the door.

Walter pushed himself to get dressed – his mother chiding him in his head about the importance of being presentable. "But it hurts, Mom," he argued out loud.

Downstairs was quiet. Gene pushed a chair back with his foot. "Hey. I was starting to think you weren't coming."

Walter sat gingerly.

"Do I need to call you a doctor or something?"

"No. I'm ok."

"As long as you don't die on me."

Walter chuckled and Gene grabbed ahold of that.

"I'd have to call your family – arrange for a coroner – and I just don't think I have the time. I mean, at least not this week. Now, next week I think I'm free."

"Oh, please. I do *not* want to be here next week."

"On this earth or… You don't mean this wonderful place?" Gene laughed. "Any news about your car?"

"They need another part. They don't know when it'll be in."

"Sorry. That's a damn shame. But hey, at least as long as you're here, you can enjoy the company."

"Looks like someone thinks too well of themselves."

"Not me, you idiot! You know well the company to which I refer."

"No," said Walter, still chuckling in hopes that he was misunderstanding.

Gene swung his arms around the room dramatically. "Nobody's here. No reason to be coy. We've all tried to imagine what it would be like with Liza. And now – *you*, little Walter - lucky dog – "

"No," Walter snapped; brows furrowed. "Absolutely nothing's happened. Not ever."

"Fine. Keep your secrets."

"There are no secrets. You couldn't be further away from the truth. Where are you getting this?"

"Hey. I was just curious. You're a private guy. I get it. I mean – not personally, but…" Gene looked up over Walters head. "Hey Liza!"

41

Walter fumed and was about to say something about a dirty trick when a little hand squeezed his shoulder.

"Hello boys."

Liza pulled the chair out next to Walter and sat down. Her hand stayed in contact with his body as she did – sliding from one shoulder to another and down his arm. Then slowly, she removed it and folded her hands together on the table in front of her. "Talking about me?"

"Of course." Gene glanced at Walter.

"You've been missed Walt," said Liza.

"He's been at deaths door."

Liza reached out. "Are you alright? Have you been having more of those nightmares?"

Walter shook his head. "Some bug."

"You should have told me Walt! I would've been able to bring you some tea or soup. You really should have said something. It's so silly that I'm right next door and you – "

"I didn't want soup," Walter interjected somewhat forcefully. "I wanted to be left alone."

Gene and Liza looked stunned for a second.

"That was not called for," Gene grunted.

"No, no Gene. I deserved it," said Liza. "I'm too

motherly for my own good sometimes. I'm sorry if I made you uncomfortable, Walt."

Walter stared down at the table. "I'm sorry, I'm not feeling well."

Liza leaped up. "Oh, of course! Poor thing! You need to get back in bed. Come, Gene, help me get him back upstairs. He looks positively ragged and here we are chiding him."

Both Liza and Gene took one of Walters arms and forced him to his feet. But because he hadn't had anything to eat or drink in nearly two days, standing suddenly made his head swim and roll back. His knees gave way and his dead weight broke his arms free of his helpers. Walter struck his head on the chair-back before his body hit the ground.

CHAPTER 7

The first flutterings of consciousness produced only impressions. Warmth on his face. Being lifted with some difficulty and his elbow scraping a door frame. Cold metal on his bare chest. Voices. Pain. So much pain in his head that he gripped and twisted the bedsheets. Once consciousness started taking a firmer foothold, he was aware that he was lying in his own scratchy bed with blankets covering his lower half and no shirt. Liza's face, hovering over his, increased in clarity. She was sitting on the bed up towards his shoulder, cradling his hand.

She smiled widely. "Well, hello there."

She leaned in closer to his face and adjusted a bandage that was partially covering one of his eyes. "You love attention Walt, don't you? Nightmares. Not eating. Concussion. You just have to be the center of attention. Well, that's alright. I'm right here for you. You don't have anything to worry your handsome little head about. You've been through so much. Being abandoned by your fiancé.

The war. Little Margery dying in your arms. It's all too, too much. Too much for you to handle on your own. You need people in your life Walt. People that care. People to take care of you."

Tears rolled down Walters swollen cheeks. "You took them."

"What are you talking about?"

"*You* – took them."

"Walt, this is the concussion talking." Liza ran her fingers down his throat and nestled them in his chest hair. "I'm here for you. Now, get some rest."

She stood and moved to the door. Walters gaze couldn't follow. His head was pounding. But he could hear Charlie's voice at the door, asking how "the kid" was doing.

"Very disoriented," said Liza.

Walter kept his eyes open for as long as he could manage, which wasn't very long. Within minutes he was lost again to time and control.

When Walter awoke again his mouth felt very dry.

"Water," he whispered.

"Here you are son," said Charlie, pouring him a glass and helping him sit up. "Slowly, slowly. I know it's good but best to take it slow."

Walter gasped, water dripping down his chin. "Thank you."

"How's your head?"

"Hurts. But, better."

"Good. Good. Good to see you awake. I mean, I know you don't really know me, but I've spent a lot of hours staring at you sleeping."

"How long has it been?"

"Almost three full days since you hit your head. You must have a mighty appetite by now. Especially since you weren't even eating before that. You should really take better care of yourself. I'm sure you must have learned that in the Army."

"Navy."

"Huh. Can't speak to what they teach you in the Navy. But in the Army, they were very strict about keeping fit. Else we'd die of disease in the trenches. I guess you didn't see much fighting in trenches."

"Not in the Navy. Not this war, either."

"We had to keep in good health. No good to anyone to be lying in bed all day."

"I will definitely work harder on taking care of myself. Was there a doctor here?"

"Oh yes," said Charlie. "Liza took care of all that. She's been doting on you hand and foot. Adhering to all of

Docs instructions. Giving you your medicine." He nodded towards the nightstand. "Of course, you haven't made it easy on her. Been fighting her like a mad cat. I've had to come in here and hold you down. You didn't try to fight me though."

Walter had stopped listening and was fixated on the medicine on the nightstand.

"What time is it?" he asked.

"7:05."

"OK – is Gene in? Can you ask him to come see me?"

As much adrenaline was coursing through Walters veins, it could not completely overtake the heaviness that pressed down on his head and eyelids. Next thing that he knew, Gene was bursting into the room far too loudly with a used napkin tucked into his collar.

"Hey! Good to see you alive. You look – well – not well."

"Please," Walter croaked, "just sit and listen. Wait! Wait. Close the door first."

"Ugh, ok." Gene obeyed, but with absolutely no sense of urgency, which frustrated Walter. "What's up?"

"I need you to help me."

"Ok. Is this some kind of deathbed confession? Oh, I know! You found some pirate booty overseas and you want to let me know where you've stashed it. Well, good news, I don't think you're numbers up quite yet, so you can keep your gold for now."

"No. I know I'm not dying. Just, please, my head is in a cloud and I just need you to help. Please, don't let Liza near. I'm not comfortable with her."

"Why on Earth?"

"I don't trust her. I'm not comfortable with her caring for me."

Gene's brows furrowed. "She's been killing herself to take care of you."

"And I appreciate the effort. But I'm not comfortable. Isn't it enough?"

"Frankly, no. You may not trust her – God knows why – but I do. She's a great gal and she's done more for you than you even remember. She didn't have to, but she did. Because that's who she is."

"You're not going to help me?"

"Help you with what? You haven't given me a single reason why you would hate her like this."

"I don't hate her."

"Then show some gratitude. She's been waiting on you hand and foot."

"Gene, please. Just listen. I wasn't comfortable with her before all this."

"Ok, now it's coming out. You made a pass at her, didn't you? And now you're not interested anymore – trying to blame her."

"No, absolutely not. She touched me and I'm not comfortable with it."

"Touched you? Where?"

"What does it matter?"

"Where, Walter?"

"Leg, chest – in a way – it was suggestive."

"What the hell?! You're insane. Everything you're saying is insane. Let me get this right. You're claiming that a beautiful woman touched you – nowhere near anything important – and you want me to kick her out for you?!"

"That's not what I – "

"That's exactly what you meant."

"No, please just listen to me." By this point Walter was breathing hard and shaking uncontrollably. His head pounded but he still managed to lift his body up slightly and emphatically before it fell back, and his eyes rolled.

Gene seemed to calm down slightly.

"I'm going to chalk this up to brain injury Walter. Get some shuteye."

"Please," Walter whispered, waving his hand

towards the medicine bottles on the nightstand. Gene misunderstand.

"I don't know anything about those. Liza's been taking care of it. Another reason you should be grateful. She's a great gal Walter."

CHAPTER 8

Another blink and it was daylight again. Charlie was back in the chair reading a newspaper.

"Charlie, please."

"Oh! You're awake again. More water?"

"No, not now. Please, please listen."

Heels clip-clopped outside the door which swung open confidentially in a second. Liza wore a deep green dress - tight and becoming. It swung around her calves as she turned to face Walter at the end of his bed.

"How is our invalid, Charlie?"

"Just coming to again."

"That's good."

Liza gave Walters foot a squeeze and smiled with

a sweet tilt of the head.

"I think it's high time we get you out of that bed and downstairs. You need to rejoin the living Walt. Charlie, would you help me?"

Liza took the lead, worming half her own body under Walters neck and shoulders in order to lift him to a seated position. The room started spinning violently, which continued until he had been forced to his feet. Powerless to stop it, his body convulsed, expelling whatever he had managed to take by mouth in the past few days.

"Walter!" Liza scolded.

After several deep breathes however the room had stopped spinning and he was feeling inexplicably better.

"Well, we'll take care of that later. Let's get him down."

Charlie obeyed and Walter didn't let on that he was feeling any kind of reprieve, allowing himself to be half-dragged downstairs, all while Liza's hands familiarly caressed his hips.

They deposited him in a chair in the lobby, partly because he had seemed to increase in weight as they came near that location.

Liza knelt in front of him. "Are you alright here for a bit?"

Walter nodded and weakly smiled.

Liza's eyes narrowed and she scanned his face for a moment before she stood and walked away with a little twirl.

As soon as her green skirt had disappeared around the corner, Walter strained to turn and look at the front desk. Joe wasn't at his post. He turned back towards the direction of the dining room. He could hear Liza's distinctive voice chatting merrily far away. Walter grabbed ahold of the arms of the chair and started slowly to transfer his weight forward onto his legs. They were weak, but he willed them to hold. After shuffling his way, trembling, to the front desk, he leaned over it to grab the phone.

The operator spoke at the slowest rate he had ever heard. He interrupted her. "Please get me the local car shop."

She put him through with an irritated puff into the receiver.

"Bernard and Sons. How can I help you?"

"Yes, my car. This is Walter Higgins. Is it ready?"

"Ugh. Well no. I'm sorry Mr. Higgins."

"Pardon me, but why not?"

"Well, I wasn't expecting your call. I put that car on the back lot."

"Why?"

"I knew, with your injuries… there was no way to tell, but it would be some time before you'd even be able to drive. I do apologize Mr. Higgins – I didn't realize that you – I'll get those parts ordered immediately."

"Wait, hold on." Walter gripped the receiver in an effort not to throw it at the wall. "When we spoke last. It was on order."

"I'm sorry sir, I hadn't put the order in before we heard about your accident."

"Who? From who?"

"I can't rightly remember. My assistant told me I think."

"From who?"

"Can't say how he heard it – someone must've phoned from the inn."

Walter dropped his face down onto the cold veneer of the desk and rested it there. "Please order it immediately. Don't call to tell me its ready. I'll be there to pick it up in three days. It. Will. Be. Ready."

The sharp little ding of the bell sounded so much louder through the wood table-top when he let the receiver fall. Existence felt heavy, and Walter wished he could let it pull him down; through the floor and into the earth where it was warm and dark and free. Joe pulled him back to reality by clearing his throat. Walter looked up and was surprised to find that Joe wasn't looking at him with the same animosity as he always had before. In its place was a kind of tentative concern. Not empathy, but the concern that anyone might feel if they were told "there's a psychopathic killer tied up in that old shed – go take a look". Walter had the sudden urge, if he had been able, to jump up on top of the desk and dance a jig – just to see the kid scramble. It brought an absent smile to his pale face which nearly elicited the same response. Tiny ray of entertainment that it was, Walter quickly realized that he needed any connection he could get.

"Joe, do me a favor. I'm not feeling so well. Can you call the doctor that's been here and ask him to come tonight?"

"Sure thing," said Joe, quietly, from several steps away.

Walter made his way back to the chair. He took that heavy feeling and shoved it deep to the center of his being. He was not going be himself or have his own thoughts that worked their ways to the surface. Hope drove him to be resolute about that. It drove him to know that he could not be Walter Higgins now if he ever wanted to be Walter Higgins again. When Liza returned, he was ready for her.

"I'm sorry, Liza."

"Oh Walt, why?"

Liza flitted down to the floor in front of him, her skirt forming a perfect circle around her.

"I've been a jackass."

"Oh, no."

"Yes, I have. And I have to apologize. You've been nothing but kind and I'm ashamed of the way that I've behaved."

Liza half stood and brushed his cheek with her knuckles. "Poor Walt! Apology heartily accepted!"

She hugged him briefly, burying his face in her chest. He swallowed Walter Higgins deeper down.

"Liza, do you think I could get some broth and help back to bed?"

"Why, of course! Let me grab the guys."

Liza went to get the broth as Charlie and Gene helped Walter back to his room. Gene never spoke except to agree to bringing a sandwich and a glass of milk once Walter was situated in bed.

Walter sat, propped up with pillows, alert and waiting. Glancing over at the medicine bottles, he pulled them closer to the edge of the nightstand and faced their labels outward.

Gene came back with the sandwich and milk first, which was just what Walter had hoped. He thanked Gene as he left, downed the milk and put the sandwich under his pillow. A minute later came Liza with a pretty tray and placed it on his lap. He slouched, and eyes half closed, he took his time sipping the broth from the spoon. Even Liza seemed to grow tired of watching him feeding himself and was standing up to go when there was a knock at the door.

"Who is it?"

"It's Doctor Hastings."

Liza opened the door for him. "We weren't expecting you this evening."

"Yes, I got a call that Mr. Higgins was feeling poorly so I came as soon as I could. How are we doing Mr. Higgins? Well you are conscious, so that's an improvement."

Walter shook his head lethargically and noticed that Gene and Joe were standing in the doorway to his room, unable to contain their curiosity. He grabbed the medicine bottles clumsily from the nightstand and waved them around.

"Doctor! I don't know if I'm taking these right!" Walter declared, slurring his speech. The bottle lids went flying and little pills scattered.

"Walt! What are you doing?" Liza scolded. "I'll get those."

"No, that's quite alright. I'll pick them up. I'm certainly glad I came," said Doctor Hastings, taking the bottles from Walter and replacing the little pills. Once he had recapped them, he frowned. "This may be your problem Mr. Higgins. There are far fewer remaining then there should be. Ms. Elisabeth – have you not been in charge of distributing his medicines?"

Liza stared ahead and her mouth opened but nothing emerged.

"Didn't you say you would be overseeing his dosages? It's one pill a piece, at most two a day. It looks as though he's been taking five times that amount."

Walter risked a glance at the audience by the door. They were entranced.

"Oh Doctor! I'm so sorry! I left them by the nightstand, and he must have been taking more when I wasn't looking. How careless of me when he's been in this condition!"

Liza looked so saddened by the realization that any confusion in that room, was instantly replaced with sympathy. Walter, meanwhile, wrestled with the heaviness that was bubbling up again.

"That's quite alright," said the Doctor. "An honest mistake. You've certainly had your hands full with this boy."

CHAPTER 9

No one bothered to acknowledge "the boy" as they made their way out. Even Liza never made eye contact or looked back after she had snatched the medicine bottles off his nightstand. Once alone, Walter pulled out his sandwich and forced himself to eat it, even though it tasted like mouthfuls of sand. At least, there would be no more accidental overdoses.

That night, he dreamt about Margery. She had come skipping down the dock, waving and calling for him insistently. She never seemed to realize that he had anything to do, or any reason to be there other than to answer questions. Walter could divine that the occasion was special however and went down to meet her. She took his hand and smiled.

"Walter, do you have a cat? I want a cat. I want a dog most of all but also a cat. Mum says no but Dad said we could perhaps if I could always finish all my chores. Well, I do and no cat."

"Maybe they're hard to come by around here."

"Not really. But most of them are mean and run away behind the rubbish bins. I want a nice house cat. Do you have a nice house cat?"

"When I was a kid, we had one."

"What was her name? If she was a girl. Was she a girl cat or boy cat? What did she look like? Was she orange?"

Their conversation continued like this for a blessedly long time. Finally, Margery turned away and told him she had to go.

"Not yet. Maybe we can talk a little longer. I could go get you a roll from the mess."

"With butter?!"

Walter laughed. "Yes, with butter."

Margery shook her head. "No, I must go home. But I'll come back tomorrow alright Walter? Wait for me!"

Even in his dream state Walter knew there was no tomorrow and there wouldn't be any point in waiting. He sadly watched as she walked into the dark of dreamless sleep and held tight to the feeling that would come flooding back as soon as the sun rose.

Liza was sitting in his room reading a book when he woke up. Initially she didn't know he was awake, which suited him. He studied her beautiful frame – head bent over her book, one leg drawn up and the other resting on the windowsill – and realized that he could no longer see her as beautiful. She was a prison guard, a judge and an executioner. But why? The why alluded him. What was the incentive? And if there wasn't one – could the simplest answer be that he was going out of his mind?

Walter stirred and Liza looked up, smiling. "Good Morning Walt! How are we feeling this morning? Any better? I'm sure you are now that you're getting the proper amount of medication. I told Charlie to keep an eye on you. But he is getting forgetful in his old age. Are you feeling like eating anything this morning?"

"A little broth?"

"Fine. Any coffee?"

Walter motioned to his stomach and grimaced as if the thought were off putting.

"I'll get some broth then. But before I go, I wanted to talk to you."

Liza sat on the bed next to his knees and propped herself up by putting a hand between them.

"When you were in and out of things, I'm sure you won't remember, but you talked about letters. Do you remember this at all?"

"I'm not sure. What letters?"

"I think you were referring to the letters you weren't able to deliver to Margery. You seemed very concerned about them. Were you? Are you?"

"No, I don't remember anything about it."

"Alright, well. I just wanted to see how you were doing in that regard." Liza gave his shin a parting rub and left to go fetch the broth.

Walter felt hungry. So hungry he thought only briefly about how certain he was that he had never mentioned the missing letters directly, even in his foggy state.

With so little food in recent days and just a sandwich the night before, he was surprised at how much he longed for bacon and eggs. Coffee seemed like some rich, heavenly drink. When Gene popped his head in the door, Walter saw his opportunity for real sustenance.

"Morning, sorry about everything before. I know you're really sick and I was a jerk. I heard that you and Liza have mended whatever lovers spat you were having. So, no hard feelings. Anything I can get for you?"

"Thanks. Yeah, everything's fine now. If there are any more sandwiches downstairs…"

"Of course!"

"Maybe two? Just in case I get hungry later."

Gene laughed. "Sure thing."

As the morning wore on and Walter drank his broth and secretly devoured his sandwiches, he could feel little surges of strength and life. His lips could form the words he meant them to and his fingers could lift a cup without trembling. Hope swelled again. If he was given any time alone, he could have tested his strength, but there was someone with him constantly. By midafternoon, he decided that he was feeling feverish, and asked for his jacket. He hugged himself and shivered which made him legitimately feel very warm. When it was Charlie's turn to watch after him, he asked for his suitcase so that he could look for a book to read – maybe it would help get his mind off of his illness. Without much trouble, he pocketed his wallet and packets of letters. Pretending to be struck by a sudden bout of sickness, Walter threw the suitcase off the bed in front of Charlie which sent his clothes and belongings flying.

The invalid swung his legs off the bed, grabbed his shoes and made for the door. He was going to run down the stairs and get outside. If he was stopped, he would drop to his hands and knees and dry heave as realistically as possible. Half-way down the stairs everything went black and he had to stop until his vision came back. He could hear shuffling from his room and Charlie behind him saying "hold on, son" in a concerned but unalarmed tone. Walter took a deep breath and kept on. The lobby was quiet. Joe was at the desk but didn't raise his head. Walter flipped up his jacket collar, hunched his shoulders, grabbed the doorknob and burst through into the outdoors.

The moment the door was shut behind him, the enemy in his mind became the building itself. His legs couldn't keep up with his breath. He made his way to the bushes across the street, expecting to hear his name shouted with every beat of his pounding heart. All he could make out was the ringing in his ears, but he imagined he could hear Liza calling, shrill and scolding.

Behind a thicker patch of bushes, Walter let himself collapse and ventured to look behind him. He couldn't see any part of the inn, not even the roof, which meant that he had made it further in this first leg of his journey than he thought he would.

Walter allowed himself to take some pride in this accomplishment and used it to give him the will to get up, which was almost surprisingly painful. He would walk through the woods and brush, off of the side of the road for a while, until it was dark, making it easier to see headlights before he could hear engines. He had calculated in his head that if he kept up a steady pace, he could get into town in about nine hours. As he walked, however, that time frame seemed to lengthen before him. He had underestimated how weak he was and how difficult it would be to fight his way through the brush. Ticks crawling up his legs and clinging to his pants necessitated frequent stops as well. It wasn't long before he realized that trying to make it into town without stopping to rest was not going to work, but he was determined to make his logic delay. Walter also hadn't considered having no food or water – or how much his stomach had gotten used to a steady supply of sandwiches and would be pining for them.

Once it was dark, Walter pushed himself to walk for a while on the open road, and it was such an easier trek, it gave him a second wind. He turned his attention away from his growling stomach by focusing intently on one leg extending in front of the other, finding ground and pushing forward. He could be hungry and tired, but his legs were still working. Every step brought him closer to town and further away from the inn. The inn full of people that loved Liza.

After an indiscernible number of steps his legs were no longer legs but wooden polls that would not bend. He couldn't feel his feet hitting the ground anymore but only that his hips were baring or not baring weight. He lost his balance on them and fell forward onto his hands before his arms gave out as well, trembling under his own weight.

There would be no more walking tonight and the thought of making a bed, which he had been planning to do, was a laughable consideration. Blackness and nausea consumed him. Before Walter entirely lost his senses, he dragged his body off of the road.

CHAPTER 10

Walter awoke to birds and sunshine and swearing. He lifted his stiff neck just enough to free one eye from the dirt and underbrush. Gene's car was parked on the road next to him and Gene was pacing back and forth, stomping and cursing at the air. Walter let out a groan as he tried to move anything. Gene stopped dead, mid-pace, and spun around towards him.

"What the hell?! You're alive?! You're alive!"

"Apparently," said Walter, forcing his aching muscles to work.

"How?! You looked – so dead. I could've sworn I just found your body."

"You did."

"You know what I mean. Here let me help you up."

"No, I've got it. I've got it." Walter used every ounce of strength he had to keep from needing Gene's help. Although he did steady himself on the car.

"What the hell happened? Liza has been worried sick about you – none of us have gotten any rest. How in the world did you end up here?"

Walter hesitated. "I – I don't know. I don't know how I ended up here."

Gene seemed to buy it. "Like you were sleep walking or something?"

"That must have been it."

"You could've killed yourself!"

"Yeah, lucky you came along."

"Yeah." Gene put his hands in his pockets. "Yeah alright, I better get you back."

"How far away are we from town?"

"Why?"

"Just wondering."

Gene shrugged. "Probably ten minutes."

Walter had to stop himself from beaming with defeatist pride. He had made it so far, but not far enough.

"Can we drive into town first?"

"I don't know…"

"We're so close, it won't take long. I just want to check on my car, then we can head back."

Gene's face tightened skeptically and then, after looking both ways on road, finally loosened. "Alright."

The men got into the car and Gene started it up. Before he pressed the gas pedal he turned toward Walter in a slightly threatening way. "If you pass out, turn funny colors or anything – I'm taking you straight back. Kicking and screaming if I have to."

"Fair enough."

This drive into town was so different from the last. The air smelt as fragrant as a particularly generous last meal. As satisfying as it might be, there is never any forgetting that the steak and potatoes, the casserole and wine are going down the throat of a dead man.

Gene stopped his car in front of the car shop and without a word, watched as Walter got out and unsuccessfully closed the door behind him. Walter left it ajar rather than to call attention to his weak state, and made his way, as upright as he could manage, into the car shop. Once inside he dropped himself into a chair.

"Sir, are you ok?" said one of Bernard's sons. "Should I call for a doctor?"

"No, just your father."

Bernard took a long time coming into the shop. Walters heart was skipping and palpitating erratically which made him feel the need to take in deep, sharp breathes. He leaned over so that his head was between his knees.

"Mr. Higgins? Are you alright?"

"Yes, my car."

"I'm so very sorry, I just haven't gotten in the part and there's only so much we can do…"

Walter breathed in and out loudly, like he was coming up for air, and the mechanic started.

"I'm sorry Mr. Higgins. Is there some way I can make it up to you? And… do you want me to call the doctor?"

"No, the telephone. Let me use the telephone."

A minute later, Gene burst through the shop door, making the little bell attached to it ring wildly. Walter was slouched over the shop desk, having just put the phone down.

"Mr. McGivern," Bernard exclaimed in relief. "Mr. Higgins seems – not well. Should I call a doctor?"

"Yeah, I know. I'll get him back and we'll figure out what to do there."

Gene grabbed ahold of Walter firmly under the arms and had to nearly carry him out to the car.

CHAPTER 11

Liza was standing on the front porch of the inn, her brows furrowed in concern and her red lips forming a perfect frown. As soon as the car stopped, she was waving her bare arms, giving commands. Someone needed to tell cook to prepare some broth, someone needed to call the doctor and others needed to carry Walter back upstairs to his room.

Walter observed these happenings in an almost passive capacity. He had nothing left of himself after his long, arduous walk. Being back in the building he had suffered so much to leave didn't give him much to cling to either.

Before long he was situated in his old bed, propped up by pillows and stripped of both his jacket and shirt. He felt cold since there was a draft that came from the window, but all he could do was pull the scratchy covers up as high as they would reach without falling back down.

A knock on the door preceded said door opening. Liza had changed into a burgundy dress, synched at the waist with a plunging neckline. She shut the door behind her with a little, healed shoe.

"Hello, Walt!" Liza chirped. She walked over to the window and closed the curtains.

"Hello Liza."

"You look awful."

"Thank you."

"You've been busy."

"Keeps me young."

"Oh, Walt!" Liza chuckled, pulling his chair up to the bed and sitting down in an elegantly relaxed posed. "You did something very dangerous."

"I did?"

"Yes, I think you know that. You could have died out there. If I hadn't sent Gene out to find you, we would have been writing home to your mother. That would have been a damn shame. How could you do that to her?"

"I'm not sure what happened. I must have been sleepwalking."

Liza lowered her eyes and nodded. "Ah, sleepwalking. That would explain it. I appreciate you trying

Walt, but I'm not sure that's what happened."

"What do you mean?"

"Charlie had a very difficult time picking up your clothes off of the floor. He has bad knees you know. He remembers that you had gotten out of bed after feeling chilled and needing your coat. Of course, you could have fallen asleep after that, thrown the suitcase and run off. But no, I don't feel that sleepwalking is the problem."

"What is the problem, then?"

"Just because I am doing everything in my power to care for you, doesn't mean that I disrespect you. I don't have the kind of derision that you might expect for a man like yourself."

"Like myself?"

"You may not be the strongest of your sex, in body or mind. But have I ever given you any indication that I had a problem with that? Remember that first night – you were having the worst night terror I had ever seen – the guys didn't know what to do with you. But I was here. Sat right here and talked you through it. Encouraged you to come clean and tell me all about Margery. I didn't even know you then, but I felt for you in your fragile state. I wanted to make sure that you were alright. I did my best to introduce you to others. To help you make friends in our little community. Everyone felt that you were too much to handle but I defended you. You couldn't help the horrible things that had happened to you or the horrible ways that those things have ravaged your mind. You must have taken my care and concern for scorn. That's one possibility at least. It makes sense why you would work so hard to leave. Risk your life like that. You felt so ashamed for having to rely on me when you thought that I couldn't respect you. Does that make sense? I know you would probably disagree, but can you at least grant that it makes sense?"

"Yes," said Walter, before he said, "No. No, it doesn't make sense. I don't care whether or not you respect me. You can hate me if you want. I didn't risk my life to leave because I care about what you think of me. I risked my life to leave because, since day one, there have been too many things piling up together that make me not trust you. Everything you do looks good but no good comes from it. I don't understand why you are the way you are. Or do the things you do. I don't know what you're after. And I don't really care. I don't trust you."

Liza stood up slowly – sadly and put a hand on her chest. "That's so – discouraging. I thought that we were friends Walt. I thought we had come to understand one another. Our conversations have meant so much to me and I thought they had meant the same to you. It's such an awful shame. I'm sorry that I have been so discomfiting when I thought I was something else. I do care about you very much Walt."

Liza paused is if to give him a chance to reply. It was a chance he did not take. She sighed, reached into her skirt pocket.

"Whatever you think of me, I'm not going to stop caring for you. You're so very sick."

"If I'm sick it's because of you."

"I'm so sorry that you feel like that Walt." She lifted up a pill and rolled it between her thumb and forefinger. "It's high time for your medicine. You haven't had any in a couple of days and the doctor will ask whenever he arrives. I am responsible for you whether you like it or not."

Walter looked at her and at the pill and shook his head.

"Oh, Walt."

Liza climbed up onto the bed beside him and jerked the pillows out from behind his head and neck. Holding the pill in her left hand, she placed her right on his upper shoulder, her thumb on his Adam's apple. Walter exerted his strength to turn away and use his forearm as a shield. She slid her thumb down to his jugular and pressed down suddenly with all her weight. Walter choked and struggled more wildly. She released his throat, grabbed ahold of his wrists and started to scream, "Help! I need help here!"

With shocking speed, five or six men burst into the room. Liza let go, panting and pointed to the bed. "He needs his medicine. Hold him."

"Gene, no!" Walter cried – a raspy, feeble cry. But Gene didn't respond. Charlie was there. And Joe. But they were all there for her. They would all do her bidding.

Every limb was pressed deep into the bedsprings

so that he couldn't feel his hands or feet. Someone worked to pry open his jaws while Liza climbed up onto his chest with her knees. He couldn't breathe.

"Walt. Don't do this," she said gently. "Don't be difficult."

CHAPTER 12

"Wally!" Came a voice from the hall. "Wally! Are you here?"

Liza and all of the men forcing Walter down, paused to listen.

"See who that is," she barked. Joe scattered to obey. He popped his head back in after a minute.

"It's his mother."

Although everyone had had enough conviction a moment before to do what it was they were doing, they seemed to inexplicably lose it all at once. Walter was released and he gasped audibly, just in time for his mother to walk into the room.

"Wally?!" she exclaimed, rushing to his side. He looked particularly bad. His chest and legs were bare, pale and splotchy, and several bruises were already developing, with a large purple one on his throat. Mrs. Higgins looked around at the stunned faces. "Please, someone fetch me water and some cool rags."

Someone became everyone. Everyone disappeared and left mother and son alone. Mrs. Higgins drew the blanket up over him and stroked his hair with her sweet-smelling hand. Feeling the sudden warmth and comfort of legitimate care was a shock to his system.

"There, there dear. I'm here. Mother's here. Oh, Wally!"

"Don't look so distressed, Mom," Walter whispered, smiling painfully. His jaw clicked when he moved it.

"I'm not. I'm just worried about you. You sounded so – not like yourself on the phone. And now to find you here like this. But you're ok now. We can talk about it later. I'm here."

"Yes. Thank you, Mom."

"Once I get you cleaned up and dressed, I'll have one of the fellows help me get you to the car and we'll be on our way to a hospital. Oh, here come the water and rags. You should try to sit up a little and sip on this."

While Walter drank, his mother gathered up his things. She laid out some clean, comfortable clothes on the bed and gingerly helped him into them. Joe, who seemed to be the only one willing to show his face, stayed nearby.

"Alright, sonny. I think we're ready to get to the

car," said Mrs. Higgins. And Joe, who had so recently been hurting him, now carefully helped Walter out of bed and down the stairs.

The heightened sense of relief that flooded over Walter gave him the strength he didn't have to walk himself out the door. He sunk down into the cushy leather seat of his mother's car and she shut the door after him with a thud.

"I need to run back in Wally. I'll only be a moment," she said and headed back.

"Why, Mom? Wait!" But she couldn't hear him. He watched her intently. Liza emerged and the two talked on the front step of the inn. His mother dropped her head a couple of times and clasped hands with Liza before turning back towards the car.

"Mom?"

"Oh, sorry! I just wanted to thank that sweet girl. She's phoned a couple of times to let me know how you were doing. She's so sorry that she didn't realize how bad off you were. But you've always been a steadfast little soldier. You've never let on when you're sick – even when you were a tiny little boy." Mrs. Higgins started the car. "Shall we go?"

Walter nodded and looked back at Liza. She was standing so tall in her burgundy dress, waving at them.

"Look Wally! You should wave."

"No," he snapped.

"Walter! That is not very nice. She seems like such a sweet, caring girl. I wouldn't' mind if you brought a girl like her home."

* * * *

Three or four seasons later, Walter got the keys to a gently used new car and went for a long drive. The wind on his face passed through his soul. Life wasn't good, but it was better.

He saw a dirt road, similar to the road he might have died on so many months before and made the turn. Here he was, healthy and well fed, in a car that could take him wherever he liked. Yes, life was better.

Down the road a little way he stopped to look at an old Victorian house. It was covered in ivy, banisters were broken and fallen over and several windows were missing glass. Clearly no one had lived there for a few years. Because of the war, maybe?

Walter grabbed his little leather suitcase and took out his packet of letters. Hugging them to his chest he got out of the car and walked up the mailbox of the old house, which was even more heavily covered in foliage. He tore some away, opened the box, and carefully placed the packet inside. After closing it again and lifting the flag, Walter brushed his hand along the curved top of the mailbox. It seemed in a moment to become a little head of jet-black hair. Two large eyes smiled up at him with deep, unbridled joy.

"Bye, Margery. I'm – so – sorry that this ugly, ugly

world doesn't have you in it anymore. But thank you. Thank you for being such a bright spot while you were here. See you around someday."

ABOUT THE AUTHOR

Jasmine Hill is a perpetual writer – always searching for the creepy, weird and real stories everywhere. She has the sweetest, sounding board of a husband, two wonderful children, two rescue dogs and a rescue cat without a tail.